Betty Bunny
Loves Easter

ILLUSTRATED BY

Stéphane Jorisch

WRITTEN BY

Michael B. Kaplan

Dial Books for Young Readers ⬥ an imprint of Penguin Group (USA) LLC

For Holly and everyone at Pippin, who found Betty Bunny,
not unlike an Easter egg, buried beneath the bramble —M.B.K.

To my Mom and Dad, for reminding the Easter Bunny
to drop by every year —S.J.

DIAL BOOKS FOR YOUNG READERS
Published by the Penguin Group • Penguin Group (USA) LLC • 375 Hudson Street, New York, New York 10014

USA / Canada / UK / Ireland / Australia / New Zealand / India / South Africa / China
penguin.com
A Penguin Random House Company

Library of Congress Cataloging-in-Publication Data
Kaplan, Michael B.
Betty Bunny loves Easter / written by Michael B. Kaplan ; illustrated by Stéphane Jorisch.   pages cm
Summary: Betty Bunny wants to be the Easter Bunny when she grows up, but is having a difficult time finding eggs during the
neighborhood Easter egg hunt.
ISBN 978-0-8037-4061-7 (hardcover)
[1. Easter—Fiction. 2. Easter egg hunts—Fiction. 3. Rabbits—Fiction.] I. Jorisch, Stéphane, illustrator. II. Title.   PZ7.K12942Beu 2015
 [E]—dc23   2013023378

Manufactured in China on acid-free paper
10 9 8 7 6 5 4 3 2

Designed by Jennifer Kelly
Text set in Julius Primary

The artwork was rendered on Lanaquarelle watercolor paper in pencil, ink, watercolor, and gouache.

Betty Bunny was a handful.

She knew this because on the night before Easter, she was hopping all around the kitchen handing eggs to her parents, her brothers, and her sister. And that's when everyone in her family said at once:

"Betty Bunny,
you are a handful."

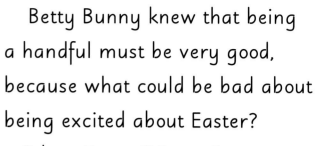

Betty Bunny knew that being a handful must be very good, because what could be bad about being excited about Easter?

"I love Easter!" Betty Bunny announced. "When I grow up, I'm going to be the Easter Bunny."

"You can't be the Easter Bunny," her brother Henry told her.

"Only the Easter Bunny can be the Easter Bunny," said her sister Kate.

"But you could grow up to be a weird bunny who runs around acting like the Easter Bunny," her older brother Bill added.

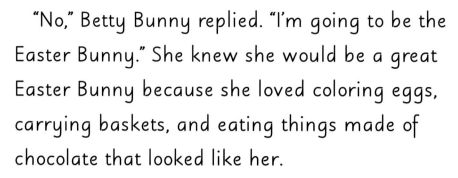

"No," Betty Bunny replied. "I'm going to be the Easter Bunny." She knew she would be a great Easter Bunny because she loved coloring eggs, carrying baskets, and eating things made of chocolate that looked like her.

She told her family that someday when she is the Easter Bunny, she will deliver baskets full of candy and toys not just on Easter, but every day of the year.

"If every day is like Easter," her mother explained, "then it won't be special anymore."

"If every day is like Easter," Betty Bunny replied, "then *every day* will be special. **You'll see.**"

The next day was Easter. After church, Betty Bunny and her
family arrived at the neighborhood park for the big egg hunt.

The egg hunt was Betty Bunny's favorite part of the day.
She was practically hopping out of her fur with excitement.

Betty Bunny's mother and father gave her a brand-new basket. It was the biggest Easter basket she had ever had.

"This is a good size," Betty Bunny told them, struggling to lift it. "I always find the most eggs, so I am sure I will fill this up." Betty Bunny took her basket and started to look.

Kate nudged an egg with her toe.
"There's one," she said.

Betty Bunny put it in her basket.

Henry shook a branch. Betty Bunny
looked over and saw that there was an
egg beneath it. "Looks like you found
another," Henry said as Betty Bunny
put it in her basket.

Bill picked up an egg and put it directly into Betty Bunny's basket.

"How do you do it?" Bill asked, sounding impressed.

Betty Bunny stopped looking for eggs. "Why are you all helping me?" she asked.

"We always help you. It's why you find so many eggs,"
Henry explained.

"I guess now you're just old enough to notice," Kate said.
"But we're not helping you *that* much," she added.

"Man, you are good at this!" Bill said, dropping three
more eggs into her basket.

"Stop it!" Betty Bunny cried out. "Easter is my favorite holiday. I'm going to be the Easter Bunny someday. I can find the eggs by myself."

"I believe in you," said Kate.

"Cool," said Henry. "Now I can go throw eggs into the basketball hoop with my friends."

"And I can go sit by the parking lot and play this egg hunt game on my phone," said Bill.

Betty Bunny dumped out all of the eggs that her siblings had found. She took her empty basket and looked for eggs all by herself.

She looked on the ground.
She looked under rocks.
She looked behind bushes.

She even looked in the
coat pocket of a lady who
did not seem at all happy
about it.

She found **one** egg.

All around her, kids were shouting, "I found one!"
"I found one more!" "I found another one!"
Betty Bunny did not find another one.

She sat down on the ground and began to cry.

Betty Bunny's mother and father came over and knelt down beside her. "What's the matter?" her mother asked.

"I hate Easter," Betty Bunny cried. "Easter is yucky." And she told her parents all about how this year she wanted to find eggs by herself, but only found one.

"I'm never going to be the Easter Bunny," she moaned.
"I'll just be a dentist. Teeth are always in the mouth, where
they're easy to find."

Betty Bunny's father told her that he was very proud of her for wanting to find the eggs by herself. It meant that she was getting to be a big girl. Her mother was proud of her too. She told Betty Bunny that it doesn't matter how many eggs she finds. Any egg she finds by herself will mean so much more than eggs that someone else gives her.

Betty Bunny nodded and wiped
away her tears. Then she began
looking for more eggs.

She found one buried
in the tall grass.

She found another
beside the swing set.

She had three eggs in her giant basket. That was all she could find.

But her mother was right. Those three eggs she found by herself meant more to her than any eggs she had ever had.

Maybe when she grew up, she would be the Easter Bunny in the spring, and a dentist the rest of the year.

That afternoon, Betty Bunny's mother saw Betty Bunny going through her purse. "Betty Bunny," she scolded, "what are you doing in my purse? That is not okay."

"I need money to buy an even bigger basket for next year," Betty Bunny explained.

"Then you need to ask me," her mother replied.

"If I ask you," Betty Bunny said, "you'll just give it to me.
It means so much more if I find it myself."